# The BOY with DINOSAUR HANDS

Written by
## Al Carusone
Illustrated by
## Elaine Clayton

## Clarion Books/New York

Clarion Books
a Houghton Mifflin Company imprint
215 Park Avenue South, New York, NY 10003
Text copyright © 1998 by Albert R. Carusone
Illustrations copyright © 1998 by Elaine Clayton

The text is set in 13/17-point Guardi.
The illustrations were executed in pen and ink and acrylic.

Printed in the USA

*Library of Congress Cataloging-in-Publication Data*

Carusone, Al
The boy with dinosaur hands / Albert R. Carusone
p. cm.
Summary: A collection of eight spooky stories, including "It Will Grow
Back Bigger," "Nightcrawler," and "The Space Behind the Piano."
ISBN 0-395-77515-9
1. Horror tales, American.   2. Children's stories, American.
[1. Horror stories.   2. Short stories.]   I. Title.
PZ7.C253Bo   1998
[Fic]—dc2          97-24616          CIP          AC

VB     10 9 8 7 6 5 4 3 2 1

*To my wife, Gwen*

—A. C.

# CONTENTS

# The **BOY** with
# **DINOSAUR HANDS**

IT WAS UNFORTUNATE that Marty tripped as he was reading the big sign on the wall of Mr. Feinster's Quick-Stop Store, downright unfortunate. What made it even worse was that he tumbled right into Rebecca D'Aliquiste, who was standing at the cosmetics rack.

Rebecca whirled around like a cyclone and stabbed her finger at Marty's nose. "Why don't you watch where you're plodding about," she admonished him. "And don't ever put those . . . those dinosaur hands on me again."

The two junior high cheerleaders standing with Rebecca tossed their perfectly coiffured heads and giggled.

Marty's hands fled into the safety of his pockets. "I'm sorry," he managed to sputter. "I was just reading the sign about the talent show." Marty nodded toward the sign, which read in bold letters, TALENT SHOW FOR BOYS AND GIRLS—BIG PRIZES

Rebecca pulled her finger away from Marty's face and coolly sheathed it in one of her lambskin gloves. "Why would *you* read a poster about a talent show? What can you do besides trip?"

Rebecca's friends glared at Marty as if daring him to have any talent.

"I don't care about the dumb old contest," Marty said. "I was just reading the sign, that's all."

"Well, it's a good thing you're not going to enter, because Rebecca is going to win," said one of the cheerleaders.

"She has real talent," added the other. "She's been on local television doing her hand shadows. She does bunnies and butterflies and babies."

With that the three girls flounced out of the store.

"You going to let them get away with that, kid?" Mr. Feinster asked Marty.

"Who cares about the talent show?" Marty said. "It's not like I want to be in show biz or anything."

"That's not the point," Mr. Feinster said. "The talent show doesn't matter. What matters is winning and losing. Do you want to be a loser for the rest of your life?"

"My dad always says winning isn't everything," said Marty.

Mr. Feinster pulled a baseball bat out from under the counter. "I always taught the boys on my baseball team to win at any cost." He tapped the bat against his beefy arm for emphasis.

"I didn't know you coached baseball," Marty said. "I play second base."

Mr. Feinster slipped the bat back under the counter. "I don't actually coach any more," he said in a hushed tone. "There was a little trouble with a certain umpire. I had taken my team all the way to the state championships. I wasn't about to let anyone stand in my way. You know how everyone's always yelling 'kill the ump'? Well, I guess I get a little bit carried away sometimes," he said with a faraway look in his eyes. "But like they say, that was then. Now we've got to win you a talent show, kid."

Marty shook his head. "I don't know."

"I'll be your coach," Mr. Feinster said, pulling off his apron. He moved his big body around the counter with surprising speed.

"What could I do in the talent show?" asked Marty.

"That's easy," said Mr. Feinster. "You'll do hand shadows like Rebecca D'Aliquiste does. Beat her at her own game."

"I can't see myself doing bunnies, even if I could do hand shadows, which I can't," Marty said, looking doubtfully at his hands.

"Of course you won't do bunnies!" Mr. Feinster shouted. "I wouldn't coach you if you did. You'll do dinosaurs."

"Dinosaurs?"

"That's right. Rebecca D'Aliquiste gave me the idea when she said you have dinosaur hands. You'll be Marty Prince, The Boy with Dinosaur Hands."

Marty liked the ring in Mr. Feinster's voice as he said The Boy with Dinosaur Hands. It made him feel important. Suddenly the excitement of show biz was bubbling through his veins. So Marty found himself signing up for a talent show he had never dreamed he would enter.

Every day Marty worked with a coach who got just a "little bit carried away" at times. But the day of the talent show finally dawned bright and clear. Trouble was, Marty didn't feel any more talented than before.

"I don't think I can go through with it," he admitted to Mr. Feinster as they drove to the auditorium.

"With these you can't lose." Mr. Feinster handed an odd-looking pair of gloves to Marty. "Just slip them on and you're a shoo-in to win, kid."

Marty pulled on the gloves. They were made of a gooey rubber and slid over his hands like a pair of raw eggs. The right-hand glove Marty recognized as *Tyrannosaurus rex*. The left was a long-necked plant-eating dinosaur. "Isn't this cheating?" asked Marty.

"Naw. It's just like throwing a bean ball in baseball. Everybody does it. Who does it hurt?"

"Maybe the guy who gets beaned," said Marty,

peeling the slimy gloves off his hands. He noticed that they left an angry red rash on his skin.

Mr. Feinster parked the car and ushered Marty into the big auditorium. The sheer number of people in the audience made Marty feel faint.

"Break a leg, kid," Mr. Feinster said, pushing Marty up the backstage steps. "Or in this case, break a finger."

Emily Ann Pitoon, the first performer, was already taking center stage. She balanced on one foot and fluttered the other leg gracefully. "I'm going to perform my classic waltz of the wounded gazelle," she told the hushed audience.

Marty shoved the gloves into his pockets and slipped behind the back curtain to watch his competition.

Sonny McGee followed Emily Ann. He was a star gymnast and hung upside down from a set of parallel bars. He went through a vigorous routine, and by the time he sprang from the bars to land lightly on his toes, the entire crowd was cheering.

As the other performers came and went, Marty dug his hands deeper and deeper into his pockets. When Rebecca D'Aliquiste took the stage, Marty realized that he had squeezed the plant-eating dinosaur glove onto his left hand.

The lights dimmed, and a spotlight shone straight onto Rebecca's hands. On the curtain behind her paraded a procession of bouncing bunnies, beautiful butterflies, and burping babies.

The crowd went wild. It was obvious Rebecca D'Aliquiste was their favorite.

With each shadow that flickered across the curtain, Marty found himself slipping on another finger of the *Tyrannosaurus rex* glove. By the time Rebecca curtsied and left the stage, the glove was drawn tightly across Marty's right hand. It fit very snugly, perhaps a little too snugly.

Marty stepped in front of a ghostly blue spotlight. He stretched the gloves even tighter across his knuckles. Then he started his show. Shadows danced across the curtain, dinosaur shadows.

Marty knew he had beaten Rebecca when a little girl in a white lace dress who was sitting in the front row cried, "I'm scared, Mommy. It's too real."

The girl's mother shushed her, but wonder and terror shone on her face, too.

Marty felt his power over the audience. They were his. He cupped one hand just so, and the *Tyrannosaurus rex* chased the lumbering plant-eater. The audience squealed their pleasure. Faster and faster, the *Tyrannosaurus rex* ran. Why, you could almost hear its cries against the blue Mesozoic skies of the curtain.

Every hand clapped for The Boy with Dinosaur Hands. Mr. Feinster was already collecting the first-prize money from the judges.

The little girl in the lacy white dress gasped as

the *Tyrannosaurus rex* caught the plant-eating dinosaur. Applause threatened to rip the very roof off the auditorium. It seemed so, so real.

It was the little girl in the front row who was the first to realize it *was* real. She knew even before Marty. She knew when her lacy white dress got splattered with red.

And as one of Marty's dinosaur hands ate the other hand, ate it right up to the elbow, the screaming started.

# The **SPACE BEHIND** the **PIANO**

THERE IS A SECRET PLACE in every house that has an air of magic about it. But you must be very young or very old to discover this enchanted place. In the Bowers' household, the magical place lay behind the old player piano in the living room.

Hilary Bowers felt the magic the moment her mother led her there. With a wave of her hand, Mrs. Bowers presented the space to Hilary. "It's all yours," Mrs. Bowers announced. "It can be your study area, or a place to keep special things. Whatever you want it to be."

Hilary hugged her mother. "It's nice to have a place I don't have to share with anyone. A place that's all my own."

But Hilary felt a twinge of guilt. She didn't mind

sharing her bedroom with her little sister. At least not most of the time. Then there was Great Gram. Great Gram didn't get around much, but she always seemed to get into Hilary's way. Even now, Great Gram was sitting in her easy chair, the one that had sagged into the exact contours of Great Gram's frail body. She was gazing into the big wall mirror, watching Hilary's every move.

"Maybe having this space behind the piano will inspire you to sit in front of the piano," said Mrs. Bowers. "You have a real talent for the piano. I hate to see you waste it."

Hilary made a single peck at the keyboard. She hoped her mother would leave soon so she could be in her little world behind the piano. But Mrs. Bowers was not one to give up. "Did you know that Great Gram had the same talent?"

"No, I didn't," Hilary said with surprise. "I never heard her play."

"It's been many years since she played," Mrs. Bowers said, "but Great Gram was a talented pianist."

"I just don't have time for the piano," Hilary said, staring across the street at Billy Jenkins. He was shoveling snow from his driveway. He was the best looking boy in school.

"But you have time to try out for cheerleading," Mrs. Bowers said, "so you can spend your time cheering for Billy Jenkins while he gets all sweaty wrestling on those disgusting mats."

Hilary drew further behind the piano as if Billy might somehow overhear them. "I'm only fourteen. Billy Jenkins doesn't even know I exist."

"Well, he will after tonight. He's coming to our New Year's party with his parents," announced Mrs. Bowers.

Hilary nearly collapsed onto the piano.

"I've got to get everything ready," Mrs. Bowers said, scurrying away before Hilary could bombard her with all the questions she wanted to ask.

Hilary glanced at her wristwatch. Two thirty. Plenty of time to get ready for the party. But first, she would move some of her things into the space behind the piano. That would give her time to plan the witty things she would say to Billy Jenkins.

Hilary made trip after trip, carrying her books, her magazines, and her CDs behind the piano. From the easy chair across the room, Great Gram watched Hilary with eyes that were far too intent. Then Great Gram turned to watch Billy Jenkins shovel snow. A smile stole onto her face. It was a strange smile.

With a magazine in hand, Hilary settled into the space behind the piano. It was three o'clock and so peaceful there. A world of her own. A quiet world, floating in time like a soap bubble.

Hilary scarcely paid attention to the scratching sound. What was it? The kitten? No, it wasn't Growl Tiger.

What then?

11

Great Gram. Yes, that was it. Great Gram was trying to get out of her chair. Hilary wondered why. Great Gram almost never left her chair.

Hilary could have gone to check on Great Gram, but instead she went back to her reading. It was only when the piano music crashed in on her that she stopped reading. She dropped the magazine.

The sound was very loud in the space behind the piano. Hilary struggled to her feet. Her legs had fallen asleep, and the blood rushing back through them prickled like tiny pins. Hilary poked her head around the piano, half expecting to see Great Gram at the keyboard.

Hilary snorted out a little laugh. Growl Tiger was the culprit. Something had made him jump onto the keyboard. Hilary set the kitten onto the floor, then checked her wristwatch. "Six fifty-four!" she cried. "I couldn't have been reading that long."

Across the room, Great Gram stared at Hilary with eyes that seemed unnaturally large.

Hilary looked at the large wall clock. It was going on three twenty. Hilary shook her wristwatch. Still running smoothly. What had caused it to suddenly race ahead more than three hours?

All at once an explanation came to Hilary that was so bizarre she just had to test it out. She strode purposefully behind the piano. Taking off her wristwatch, she plopped it down where she had been sitting. Growl Tiger starting playing with it, batting it with one paw. Hilary tried to coax him out from behind the piano, but the kitten wouldn't leave its newfound toy.

Hilary opened her piano book, turned to the song she was supposed to practice, and played it.

As she finished, she felt quite silly. After all, what did she expect? She didn't really think the wristwatch would leapfrog over another couple of hours, did she?

Hilary closed her piano book and peered into the space behind the piano. Her heart pounded like a runaway metronome.

Toward her walked Growl Tiger on stiff legs. He was quite grizzled with age. From a kitten, Growl Tiger had suddenly become an old cat. Hilary did not even bother to look at the wristwatch. Years, not mere hours, had passed behind the piano—passed with the playing of a single song.

Hilary gathered Growl Tiger into her arms and wept. She ran to her mother. "Look at Growl Tiger," Hilary said. "Look how old he is."

Mrs. Bowers kept at her party preparations with scarcely a look at Growl Tiger. "Hilary, I really must get these decorations up," she said, stringing a streamer of silver crepe paper from the ceiling. "If you're not going to help, then at least practice the piano. I heard you a little while ago, and you were doing fine."

Hilary clutched Growl Tiger tightly to her chest and spun around. Something was going on, and it had to do with the space behind the piano. Hilary was going to get to the bottom of it.

It was when she walked past the mirror that Hilary saw what the piano had done to her. She looked seven years old.

Her first thought was what sixteen-year-old Billy Jenkins, who had hardly noticed her as a fourteen-year-old, would think now.

Hilary sat down on the piano stool with Growl Tiger nestled on her lap. "Let's see," she said to Growl Tiger. "You walked across the keyboard when I was behind the piano, and my wristwatch jumped ahead three hours. Then when I played the song in my piano book, you got old and I got younger. I know it happened, but my mother looked right at me and didn't notice that anything had changed. Apparently you have to be either sitting in front of the piano or in the space behind the piano to remember the way things were before the piano changes them."

As Hilary struggled to piece together just what had happened, her thoughts were becoming strangely murky, as though her mind was becoming that of a seven year old. A shudder rippled through her as she realized that half of her life had been rolled back like an old carpet. And she was rapidly forgetting that part of her life.

Hilary's voice dropped to a hushed whisper. "If I can just remember enough algebra, I can figure out exactly how much piano playing it takes to change time one year. Then I can turn you back into a kitten again. And me . . ."

Hilary smiled out the window at Billy Jenkins. "Me, I can turn into a girl of sweet sixteen. Just right for Billy Jenkins."

Hilary got paper and a pencil and opened her piano book to the song she had played. Very carefully, she timed each stanza of the song. She figured out just the right amount of playing that would make her sixteen.

Hilary searched the scrolls on top of the player piano. Each would play a song when it was inserted into the piano. Each was marked with a time, the exact length of the song it played. Hilary took down one song that was the right length. The song was "Oh! Susannah."

She set the scroll into the piano, started the song, and stepped behind the piano. Growl Tiger was asleep on the piano stool. Hilary thought that was good. But she couldn't remember why it was good for Growl Tiger to be in front of the piano. Something about age. But Hilary's memory was fading fast.

Hilary sat behind the piano. The strains of "Oh! Susannah" began to wash over her like soothing bath water. The space behind the piano was such a cozy place to relax.

"Hilary!" called Mrs. Bowers. "The first guests will be arriving soon." Mrs. Bowers stomped in and out of the living room. "Where is that girl?" she muttered.

Hilary did not answer her mother. Little waves

that weren't exactly music were rippling through her in two-quarter time.

An odd sound intruded on the peacefulness. A heavy shuffling sound. Something was moving slowly, like a slug creeping through a garden. But as Hilary gained back her lost years, the sound became unimportant. Memories flooded back into her. Hilary tested her muscles. She could not yet move. But that was no cause for alarm. The song would soon be over. Plenty of time to move then. Time to dance with Billy, walk with him in the new-fallen snow.

The shuffling sound reached the piano stool. "Oh! Susannah" was winding down to the end. With a sudden scratch of protest, the scroll was yanked from the player piano. Growl Tiger gave a wail of protest as he was shoved off the piano stool.

Unsteady hands began to play the piano. Hilary tried to move, but the spell of the rippling music held her tight. Then, as the music jagged on, the hands that played it grew stronger and surer. They were talented hands, and the music was incredibly sweet.

The playing went on way too long. Hilary felt the years piling up on her like layers of dust on antique furniture. When the music finally crashed to a stop, the sounds of the party were already wafting in from the room outside.

"That was good. Play another song," someone was saying.

"Not now," answered a vibrant voice. "I want to dance with Billy Jenkins."

Behind the piano, Hilary struggled to her feet. She managed to stumble out into the living room. Strobe lights washed over the merry faces of the partygoers. Music boomed from a stereo. People were eating, laughing, dancing.

When Hilary saw the beautiful girl of sweet sixteen dancing with Billy Jenkins, she recognized her at once. Recognized her from the faded photographs in the photo album. The girl was Great Gram.

A woman pointed to where Hilary had collapsed into a bunch of party balloons. "Someone help her," the woman cried.

Mr. and Mrs. Bowers carried Hilary to the easy chair by the window. The contours of the chair seemed to fit Hilary's body perfectly.

She opened her eyes. The partygoers stood watching her. Great Gram, young and radiant, had already gone back to dancing with Billy Jenkins. She hardly seemed to realize that Hilary existed.

Hilary looked into the mirror on the wall. She realized that the incredibly old face staring back at her was now her own. In helpless rage, she watched Great Gram dancing without a care in the world.

Hilary's face wrinkled into a smile. This had happened before. This changing of places had been going on in a never-ending cycle, but she had the advantage now. She was the one who remembered.

Growl Tiger jumped into Hilary's lap. "I just know Great Gram will love the space behind the piano," Hilary told the kitten. "I hope she goes there very soon."

Hilary petted Growl Tiger's soft fur and patiently waited.

# IT WILL GROW BACK BIGGER

**D**R. FRANKS FINISHED taking Jeremy's temperature, picked up a stubby pencil, and jotted down the reading on a curly-edged medical chart. Then with a satisfied scowl, he handed Jeremy's mother a prescription for medicine.

"It may itch for a while, but be careful not to scratch that scab off." Dr. Franks, who seemed to labor under the delusion that all his patients were five years old, paused in his medical counsel to give Jeremy a lollipop. "If the scab breaks off, it will grow back bigger."

Jeremy examined the scab. It had formed in the crevice between his thumb and the rest of his hand. The scab was the size of a large garden pea. But instead of being green, it was the same color as Jeremy's skin. Dr. Franks was right about one thing—it did itch.

21

Jeremy's mother looked doubtfully at Dr. Franks. "Perhaps you should bandage the scab," she said. "Jeremy is a very *active* boy. I don't think he can go even a minute without scratching that scab. Why, he can't even sit through a day at school or a trip in the car like most children."

Dr. Franks shook his head. "We don't want to take any chances. It's best to give it plenty of air. Very peculiar scab. It looks like chickenpox, but it isn't. For want of a better name I'm going to call it peoplepox." Dr. Franks slapped a sticker on Jeremy's shirt that said SUPERDUPER LITTLE PATIENT.

They left Dr. Franks's office, and Jeremy followed his mother to the car. The first thing he did, even before he buckled up, was to rip off the sticker. He crumpled it into a big, sticky ball and jammed it into the ashtray.

Twice on the ride to the drugstore and once again on the way home, Jeremy's mother caught him trying to scratch the scab. "Don't forget what the doctor said," she warned him.

When they got home, Jeremy's mother poured a dose of gooey medicine into a spoon. Jeremy slurped it down.

"That should help," his mother said.

But the medicine did not help. The scab continued to itch. Jeremy ran into the bathroom and tried to stop the itching. The scab itched no matter what he did. It itched when Jeremy poured cold water on it. It itched when he blew hot air from his mother's hair dryer on it. It itched when he stood. It itched when he sat. It itched and itched and itched.

Finally, Jeremy could take it no more. He tiptoed to the medicine cabinet and got a cotton ball. Gently, he scratched the scab with the cotton ball. The scab kept itching, but it was as if somebody had turned down the itch volume ever so slightly. Jeremy scratched harder. The itching faded a bit more.

And then with a little pop, the scab broke off and rattled into the sink. The itch had gone away.

Jeremy picked up the scab and examined it. It was crunchy to the touch and very light, fragile as ash.

"Jeremy! You aren't scratching your scab, are you?" demanded his mother, pounding on the bathroom door.

Jeremy mashed the scab into a gritty powder and washed it down the drain. He threw open the bathroom door and strode boldly past his mother, carefully keeping his hand out of sight. "Can't a guy go to the bathroom in peace?" he said in a huffy tone.

Jeremy went quickly to his room. The spot where the scab had been was not itchy in the least. Jeremy felt good inside. He had put one over on his mother and the doctor.

But the next morning when Jeremy woke up, the first thing he noticed was the itching. It was back, worse than ever. Jeremy lifted his hand and gasped.

The scab had returned, and just as Dr. Franks had warned, it was bigger. The scab was now nearly the size of a tennis ball.

Jeremy heard his mother's footsteps heading toward his room. He could not let her see the monstrous scab. She would know he had scratched it. Then she would get mad.

In desperation, Jeremy broke off the new scab. Even though it was much bigger, it was as light as the old one. He quickly stuffed it under his bed.

"Let's take a look at your scab," said Jeremy's mother as she spooned another dose of medicine into his mouth.

Jeremy dutifully held out his hand.

"Almost gone," said his mother. "Now, aren't you glad you listened to Dr. Franks and didn't scratch it?"

Beads of cold sweat popped out on Jeremy's forehead. His mother had just said *almost gone.* Jeremy looked at his hand. The scab was already starting to grow back. It was about half its original size. To his mother it looked like the scab was shrinking, but Jeremy knew the terrible truth: It was growing back faster than ever.

That morning Jeremy, who was usually a good eater, skipped breakfast. He piled glumly into the school bus and hunched down in a seat by himself. He would listen to the doctor now. He would not break off the scab again.

But by the time the bus reached the school, the

scab was nearly the size of a football. Jeremy had to hide his hand in his gym bag. Within minutes the scab filled the bag.

The bell rang. Jeremy's first class was gym. Mr. Pulaski, the gym teacher, was a tough customer. Once, he had given Jeremy a failing grade because Jeremy had sprained his ankle. Mr. Pulaski was not the type who would put up with giant scabs on his students.

Jeremy had no other choice. He tore off the scab and rolled it across the gym floor, where it bounced into the basketballs and settled there, looking very much like just another basketball.

It was during third period that Jeremy finally went to the school nurse. She immediately called Jeremy's mother. By the time Jeremy's mother got to the school, the scab on Jeremy's hand was almost as big as Jeremy himself.

As his mother bundled him and his scab into the car, Jeremy kept blubbering over and over again, "I won't scratch it ever again, I promise, I promise, I promise."

On the way to the doctor's office, the scab began to get heavier. Just an ounce or two at first. Then pound by pound it started to pack on the weight. By the time they reached the doctor's office Jeremy and the scab looked like twins.

Dr. Franks strapped both Jeremy and the scab onto the examining table. "How do you feel?" he asked Jeremy.

"Lightheaded," Jeremy managed to gasp.

"I'll have to remove the scab," Dr. Franks said. "Later, I'll try to stop it from growing back."

Dr. Franks sliced off the scab, and that's when Jeremy's mother fainted. For the scab lay there just as hale and hearty as a scab can be, looking more like Jeremy than ever. It was Jeremy who floated lightly off the table and crumbled away on the floor.

# BEHIND the
# SENDING DOOR

THE TWO DOORS WERE IDENTICAL. They lay at the bottom of a crumbling set of concrete steps. Green moss covered the steps like plush carpeting.

Josh passed the round-topped doors every day on his way to and from school. Never had he seen anyone enter or leave through them. There was something gloomy about the sunken alcove, and the doors gleamed out of their dark recess like the pale eyes of a lurking snake.

Josh quickened his pace, and his friend Ronnie matched him step for step. They were halfway past the sunken doors when the first big raindrops splattered on them like water balloons.

"My project," screeched Ronnie, as he frantically stuffed the poster board map under his shirt. "The rain will ruin my map of Europe, and Mr. Biggans will flunk me."

The skies, as if in mischievous conspiracy with Mr. Biggans, opened up, and the rain fell harder.

Josh pushed Ronnie down the steps and into the alcove. There they looked out at the rain that was now falling in sheets.

"Maybe it won't last," Josh said hopefully.

Ronnie pulled the large map from under his shirt. He regarded it and gave a pained sigh. "Too late. Italy's bleeding into the Mediterranean Sea."

Josh glanced at the map. Italy, which had been traced in red, looked like a foot badly in need of medical attention.

"And just look at Eastern Europe," moaned Ronnie. "All the borders are blurred. Mr. Biggans is going to accuse me of trying to start World War Three. And I guess this rain pretty much cancels your baseball game tomorrow, too."

Josh huddled close to one of the doors. "Steady drizzle, game will fizzle," he said, quoting Coach Hernandez. "But hard rain, soon will drain."

But even as he spoke the words, Josh realized that this particular hard rain showed no sign of letting up. It seemed bent on putting Coach Hernandez out of the weather-forecasting business.

"We could knock on one of these doors," suggested Ronnie. "Maybe call someone to come and get us."

Josh looked doubtfully at the doors. "I don't know," he said. "It doesn't look like anyone uses them."

Ronnie kicked a clump of mud off one shoe.

"Every door has to lead somewhere. Besides, what have we got to lose?"

"Which door should we try?" asked Josh.

Ronnie shrugged. "How could it matter?"

Josh felt a little silly, but he studied the doors for a long second before he picked one and knocked. Three loud raps.

"Probably no one here," he said.

But it did not take long for the door to lurch open with just the sort of creepy groan that a door in a scary movie might make. Josh felt his heart kick-start in his chest, revving up like a motorcycle engine.

*Run!* The word had not been spoken. It popped out of Josh's thoughts like a jack-in-the-box.

And Josh almost did run.

*Ridiculous.* This word painted itself over the first in the more sensible part of Josh's brain. After all, what could be dangerous about a door opening in response to a knock? A door in a drab brownstone building, in broad daylight, no less.

The old woman who slowly emerged from the doorway looked like someone's favorite grandmother. She was plump, with the kind of twinkle in her eyes that said she liked to bake chocolate chip cookies and serve them up with plenty of cold milk.

"Yes?" said the old woman in a voice that was terribly thin and quite unlike the rest of her. "What brings you to the sending door?"

29

"Sending door?" asked Josh. He distributed his weight evenly across both feet in response to the thin voice, like when he wanted to steal a base in a baseball game. This gave him the option of going both ways, depending on what the pitcher did.

"Don't they teach you young folks to read these days?" the woman asked, pointing to a small brass plate at the very top of the door.

"What's a sending door?" asked Josh. He was sure the sign had not been there before. He shifted his weight, ready to run back to the safety of first base should the old woman try a pick off play.

The woman came closer. Her clothes smelled faintly of some spice that Josh's mother kept in her spice cupboard. Not a common spice, but one of the spices that sat, unused in the back of the cupboard, year after year.

"This is the door where wishes are sent out into the world," the old woman said. "Make any wish and it will come true."

Ronnie snorted in disbelief.

Josh studied the old woman. She looked so sure of herself that he felt she could not be lying.

Josh shifted his weight toward the woman. On a whim, he said, "I wish the rain would stop. And I want to hit three home runs in tomorrow's game." He looked at Ronnie who stood, wordlessly opening and closing his mouth like a goldfish. "Oh yeah," Josh added. "I want Ronnie to get an 'A' on his geography project."

The old woman drew herself back into the doorway. "It is done," she said. With that, the door slammed shut in Josh's face.

Ronnie nudged Josh with an elbow. "Look behind you," he said, and his voice held just a touch of awe.

Josh turned around slowly. He expected, yet did not expect, what he saw. The sun blazed brightly. Only a few scattered puddles remained from the rain, and these were already soaking into the ground.

"You don't suppose—" Josh started to say.

Ronnie shook his head. "Of course not. Coincidence, that's all." He held his map up for Josh's inspection. "My map didn't change. See. It's still a mess."

"Well, if I hit three home runs in tomorrow's game, you'll be a believer," Josh said. "That would be two out of three wishes."

"Fat chance of that," Ronnie grumbled, leading the way up the steps. "Considering the fact that you're just a benchwarmer."

But Josh could not get the sending door out of his mind. Even as he bent over to lace up his baseball spikes the next day, he thought about it.

He didn't see Rawley Towers sneak up behind him.

Rawley, who was the biggest and meanest kid in the school, snapped a towel with a ferocious crack at Josh's backside. "Gotcha!" Rawley cried gleefully.

Josh shot straight forward, landing heavily against the locker in front of him. A few guys started to laugh, but quit when Coach Hernandez peeked around the row of lockers. The coach scowled at Rawley, who padded back to his own locker, looking very innocent.

"Let's move it," called Coach Hernandez. "We're playing the first-place team. We need the right attitude to beat them."

The team streamed out of the locker room. Coach Hernandez stopped Josh and Rawley. "I'm penciling you in on the roster today, Josh. Rawley, you're on the bench."

"Why?" growled Rawley. "I'm ten times better than this punk."

"Attitude," replied the coach. "I like Josh's; I don't like yours." Coach Hernandez gave Josh an encouraging slap on the back.

The moment Coach Hernandez was out of sight, Rawley grabbed Josh and spun him around. "I hope you don't have plans for dinner tonight," he said, balling his big hand into a fist. "I'll be treating you to a filet-of-knuckle sandwich."

Josh tore away from Rawley and sprinted onto the field. He had a game to play.

Just after Josh hit his second home run, Ronnie jumped down from the bleachers and joined him at the bench.

Ronnie's eyes blazed. "I did it," he said.

"Did what?"

"I got an 'A' on my map project."

"But your map was smeared," said Josh.

"Mr. Biggans loved it," said Ronnie. "He said I showed real sensitivity to the pollution in the Mediterranean and to the rapid changes engulfing Eastern Europe."

Josh whistled softly. He whistled louder when he hit his third home run of the game.

On the way home after the game, neither Josh nor Ronnie spoke of the sending door. But Josh knew it weighed just as heavily in his friend's thoughts as it did in his own.

When they reached the moss-covered steps, Ronnie peered furtively about. "Let's go down," he whispered.

"I don't know if we should," Josh said.

"We've got to," insisted Ronnie. "That door made you the star of the game. It got me an 'A' from Mr. Biggans. We've just scratched the surface when it comes to wishes." Ronnie pulled out a long handwritten list from his pocket.

Josh put up a hand in protest. "Maybe there's a catch somewhere," he said.

Ronnie started down the steps. "I'm starting at the top of my list, with or without you." He raised his fist to knock.

"It's the other door," said Josh, joining Ronnie. "But you have to keep it down to one wish."

Ronnie moved over to the other door. "One wish each then," he said, knocking briskly.

The woman with the plump body and thin voice opened the door. "My, my," she said. "More wishes already?"

"You bet," said Ronnie, scanning his list. "I think I'll go for a million dollars."

Josh grabbed Ronnie's arm. "Don't get greedy. That much money's bound to get the wrong kind of attention."

"All right then," Ronnie said with an impatient stamp of his foot. "I wish for a hundred dollars."

Immediately Ronnie was holding a crisp one-hundred-dollar bill in his hand.

"Might be counterfeit," said Josh suspiciously.

"Don't be silly," Ronnie said. "My 'A' wasn't counterfeit, and neither were your home runs. Go on, make a wish."

Josh gave in and wished for a hot dog and a root beer—on the condition that Ronnie make no more wishes that day.

The old woman handed Josh his hot dog and root beer, then gently closed the door.

The hot dog smelled delicious, but Josh never got a chance to taste it. As he reached the top of the steps, there stood Rawley Towers.

"Where did you get the food?" Rawley asked, shoving Josh. Without waiting for an answer, Rawley grabbed the hot dog and gulped it down. He reached for the root beer next, but suddenly noticed the hundred-dollar bill fluttering in Ronnie's hand.

"Wow!" said Rawley.

He made a grab for the money. Ronnie held on, and the bill tore in half. Rawley quickly punched Ronnie in the face. One punch and Ronnie gave up his half of the bill.

Josh dropped his can of root beer and caught Ronnie before he pitched down the steps. Root beer spilled over the moss-covered steps, puddling into little pools with foam caps.

Rawley raised his fist again. He took two menacing steps forward. "You guys are onto something here, and you're going to let me in on it. Or else." Rawley grabbed Ronnie and began shaking him so hard that Ronnie's head tossed about like a coconut in a hurricane.

"Where did you get the money?" Rawley demanded.

Once again Josh felt the urge to run, to save himself. But he could not abandon Ronnie.

"There's an old woman behind the door who gives you anything you want," Josh said. "Now stop hurting Ronnie."

Rawley let go of Ronnie and started down the steps. "You better not be lying," he said, kicking the root beer can out of his way.

"He's not," whimpered Ronnie.

Josh opened his mouth to tell Rawley he was knocking at the wrong door when the door swung open. A very thin old woman appeared at the door. She was little more than skin and bones.

"Welcome to the receiving door," she said in a voice that was altogether too hearty for her body. And it struck Josh that this woman had the voice that by rights the plump woman at the other door should have had. It was as though the women had, through some cosmic mix-up, been born with each other's voice.

Rawley stumbled back a step, with a look on his face that showed he knew something was terribly wrong.

Josh glanced up at the brass plate at the top of this door. RECEIVING DOOR it said. Because he glanced up, he did not fully see the tube that shot out of the woman's mouth, the tube that was far too small for Rawley Towers to pass through. That, however, is precisely what happened! Rawley Towers was sucked right through the tube and into the woman at the receiving door. But the very worst part was when the thin woman made a satisfied slurping sound. The sort of sound that the last bit of a tasty milk shake might make as it's sucked through a straw.

# The DJIN-JUM MAN

THE FOOTSTEPS RUSTLING IN THE LEAVES behind Colin Hatfield did not cause him any alarm at first. Oh no, not at first.

Colin whistled as he kicked his way through the heaps of nutty-smelling brown leaves piled along the narrow walkway. Plumes of broken leaves rustled around his boots with each step. Gritty leaf dust coated the inside of his nose, tickling his nostrils with a fragrance that didn't quite smell good and didn't quite smell bad.

Colin walked a little faster and whistled just a little louder. After all, he was a famous man. Well, sort of famous. He had done something no one else could ever do. He had done it even though it was a bad thing to do. Behind Colin, the rustling footsteps faded.

But when Colin slowed his pace, the footsteps were still there. They kept coming with a steady rustle, rustle. Colin turned to the left. The foot-steps turned to the left. Colin veered to the right. The footsteps veered to the right.

Ahead was the sleepy New England village where Colin was staying. The quaint buildings creaked in a sudden squall as if trying to dodge the heavy wind on limbs that were much too old to do it nimbly. Leaves swirled and twisted about like people on a dance floor. Dust choked Colin.

The footsteps stayed stubbornly behind Colin, never speeding up, never slowing down. Colin stopped and turned slowly. His breath whistled like a long confetti streamer into the frosty air. Not twenty steps behind him walked a man with a face as blurry as swirling leaves. The man's arms pumped up and down with every step. He was a man Colin had seen many times before. He fol-lowed Colin with a steady and tireless pace.

Colin broke into a sweat and a run at the same time. By the time he lurched into the old hotel where he was staying, the man with the blurry face was nowhere to be seen. But Colin knew he was coming, following at that frighteningly steady pace.

"What is the matter, Mr. Hatfield?" James, the desk clerk, asked. "You look all done in."

"I have to check out at once," Colin said, heav-ing a sigh heavy as the rumbling of boulders. "Someone has followed me here from Tasmania."

"But you flew in, sir," James reminded Colin.

"And the airport has been closed since your arrival due to the coming storm. How could anyone have followed you?"

"He didn't fly," Colin answered as he looked outside. Already the first snowflakes were falling.

"Ah, someone drove him into town then?" James persisted.

Colin steadied himself against the front desk. "No, he walked. It used to take him days, even weeks to catch up with me. But now he's found me in twelve hours."

James snorted in disbelief. "Really, sir. I don't mean to be rude. But it's not humanly possible for a man to walk from Tasmania to Massachusetts in twelve hours."

Colin glared at the insolent desk clerk. He dabbed his dry tongue at his drier lips. "It's no human being that follows me. It's the Djin-Jum man."

James looked as if he wanted to snort again. But he held back. "If I may be so bold as to ask, sir. Who is this Djin-Jum man? And why does he follow you?"

Colin again looked outside. The town was like a picture postcard. He shivered, even though the hotel was overly warm. "It happened right after I shot the tiger," he explained. "The old woman in the Tasmanian village said that by killing the last tiger, I would call the Djin-Jum man upon myself." Colin shivered again, more violently this time. "She was right."

40

James snorted once, twice. His heavy jowls quivered as he fought back laughter. "I do believe you are putting me on, sir," he managed to say at last. "I am somewhat of a student of geography. And let me assure you, there are no tigers in Tasmania."

"That is because of me, you buffoon," Colin said, hammering the desk register with his fist and making papers flutter into the air. "I am Colin Hatfield, the man who shot the last of the Tasmanian tigers. And because of it, a terrible curse was placed on me."

James hastily gathered the papers that Colin had scattered across the front desk. He kept his gaze low. When he spoke again, it was in a meek tone, as if he were addressing a great person—or a crazy person. "Shall I call you a cab, sir?"

Colin nodded. As James dialed the telephone, Colin again licked his parched lips. He searched his pockets for a stick of chewing gum.

James hung up the phone. "With this weather, it will be over an hour before they can get here," he said.

Colin marched to the door. "That's fine. In the meantime, I'm going to the little store down the street for some chewing gum."

"Do be careful, sir," James shouted as Colin stomped out into the swirling snow.

Colin fought his way through the thickening storm. Behind him, he thought he heard the hotel door open, then slam shut again. He looked back, but could see nothing.

Snow pelted Colin's face. The little store was only a block and a half away, but it took Colin a long time to reach it. Luckily, it was still open. Colin slid some change onto the counter and took his gum. He started back to the hotel, wondering how soon the taxi would be there. After all, he still had to pack his bags.

Shoving a stick of gum into his mouth, Colin picked up his pace. The decision to walk fast on the slippery sidewalks was not a good one. He lost his footing and crashed into the unyielding hardness of a fire hydrant. He spun around backwards as he fell and banged the curb with the back of his head.

Colin lay stunned. His arms and legs had gone numb. He struggled to move them. The gum caught in his throat. He coughed it out. Snow caked his mouth, and Colin wondered how something made of water could taste so dry and powdery.

Behind the shadowy screen of the falling snow came a darker shadow. Colin strained to see. His limbs tingled with warmth. Soon he would be able to move, but for now he lay helpless.

The Djin-Jum man emerged into the light of the overhead streetlight. Step by step, he approached Colin. Six steps away, five, four, three . . .

Colin struggled to move. He could feel his fingers and toes now. In just a second, he would be able to run.

But in a second it would be too late. The Djin-Jum man was upon him. Colin looked up into the face of his pursuer. In the dull yellow glare of the street lamp, it seemed the face was taking on more definite features.

Colin was able to raise one hand to fend off the Djin-Jum man. Something stung the hand, then rolled off. It was only the gum foil that Colin had discarded. The wind had whipped it back at him. His breath froze into powder drier than the snow.

And then the Djin-Jum man walked right past Colin without even glancing at him.

Colin's breath melted back into sweet, breathable air. He managed to scramble to his hands and knees. He looked at the retreating legs of the Djin-Jum man. That's when a peculiar detail caught Colin's attention.

Two sets of footsteps stretched between him and the store. One was fresh, made by Colin on his way back to the hotel. The other set was nearly covered with snow. It was in this set of footprints, those faded indentations heading toward the store, that the Djin-Jum man tread. The Djin-Jum man tread exactly in the footsteps Colin had made, footstep for footstep.

Colin jumped up in excitement. Carefully but quickly he scampered back to the hotel. "The Djin-Jum man walked away from me. He could have gotten me, but he didn't," he shouted to James. "Do you know what that means?"

James stood silently behind the desk. His face was as white as the falling snow. He trembled as though within him raged a wind as hard as that outside the hotel doors.

"I'll tell you what it means," Colin continued. "It means you were right to snort at me. I was a fool. The Djin-Jum man is no longer following me."

"S-sir," James stammered. "I don't mean to contradict you. You being a paying customer and all. B-but I'm afraid I shouldn't have snorted. You see, sir, the Djin-Jum man *is* following you. He followed you in here just after you left to get your chewing gum."

Colin stared at the frightened desk clerk, and a terrible realization came to him. "The Djin-Jum man didn't get me in the snow because he was following the footsteps I had made *to* the store. But by now he is on the way back, following the other set of footsteps."

Just then the knob on the front door turned. Colin bounded up the steps. Suddenly the lights flickered. All was darkness for a second, then light washed back over Colin. He sprang into his room, grabbed a single suitcase, and stuffed clothes into it pell-mell.

There was a stirring at the door. Colin walked in a zigzag pattern through the room. "That should slow him down awhile," he said aloud.

The door creaked open. Colin stepped to one

side. He hoped he was not standing where he had first stepped into the room. For that would be where the Djin-Jum man would enter. Colin pressed himself hard against the wall. Surely he would be safe there.

The Djin-Jum man stepped into the room. He passed so close to Colin that Colin could feel the man's cool breath on the back of his neck.

Colin slid forward and slipped out of the room. The Djin-Jum man was already walking the zigzag course Colin had laid. He seemed to be moving faster.

Colin slammed the door shut and rushed downstairs.

"Taxi's ready," said James.

Colin dashed outside and got into the taxi. The driver nonchalantly pulled the flag down on the meter. "Where to, buddy?"

The door of the hotel was already opening. "Anywhere!" Colin cried. "But hurry!"

The cab driver shrugged his shoulders. He continued his preparations as though in slow motion. The Djin-Jum man walked toward the cab.

Colin gripped his suitcase. He was ready to bolt out the opposite door if necessary. The Djin-Jum man leaned toward the window. He pressed his face into the glass like an eager kid looking through the window of a candy store. Colin saw the face clearly, saw it for the first time.

The cab sped off.

"Where to, buddy?" the cab driver repeated.

But Colin did not answer. He knew now he could never hope to escape the Djin-Jum man. For the face Colin had seen pressed against the window was not that of a horrible monster or a powerful spirit. The face he saw was his own.

# The FUNHOUSE PEOPLE

IT HAD SEEMED LIKE it was going to rain during the entire drive to the amusement park. The clouds, hanging gray and sodden across the sky, were playing a teasing game of "will-it-rain-or-won't-it?" One minute, they would gobble the sun out of the sky and spit rain onto the windshield. The next, they would spit the sun back out to quickly dry up the raindrops.

But by the time Brian Redding and his family reached the park, the clouds had finally tired of their game and spun off like wisps of cotton candy, leaving the big orange sun alone in the sky.

Mr. Redding pulled the car into the parking lot. "Who's ready for some lunch before we hit the rides?" he asked.

Brian and his mother stirred slowly from the car, like big insects testing wet wings. But Brian's little brother Davey tore out of his seat. "I want French fries smothered with ketchup," he said, already running toward the twin Ferris wheels that towered in the distance.

Brian and his parents hurried to catch up.

Davey skidded to a stop in front of the food stand. Brian picked his way carefully over the sticky residue of a spilled snow cone and stepped over a discarded hot dog bun.

The food stand was a rude, cement-block affair, but mouthwatering food smells wafted from inside. Brian selected a table that faced the rides, while his parents and Davey went to the counter to order the food.

Seated a few tables away were three skinny boys who seemed to be Brian's age. Well, they weren't actually seated. Not all the time anyway. They hopped in and out of their seats, traded chairs, and pushed and shoved one another. Their hair was wild and unkempt. Brian had a sinking feeling in his stomach the minute he saw them.

Mr. and Mrs. Redding rejoined Brian, setting two large trays of food on the table. Davey noticed the three boys and waved enthusiastically at them. "Hello!" he said. "Would you like to sit with us at our table?"

"Don't talk to *them*," cried Brian in a voice that was louder than he expected it to be.

"You're not being selfish, are you, son?" asked Mr. Redding, motioning the boys over to the table.

The three boys filed to the table, heads bent.

"We didn't do nothing," one said. "You got nothing on us."

Mr. Redding smiled at the boys. "No one claims you did. How about some pizza?"

The boys looked at the pizza. Brian thought he saw a gnawing hunger in their eyes, but it was not a hunger for food.

Davey grabbed a piece of pizza, burned himself on the pan, and let the piece fall in a gooey pile on the floor.

Mrs. Redding started to scold him.

One of the boys stared at her. "Who do you think you are, talking to him that way?" he said.

"I think I'm his mother," Mrs. Redding said, aghast at the boy's tone of voice.

"Well, we don't want your pizza," said the boy.

"We gotta go," said the tallest of the boys. "They're waiting for us."

"Who's waiting for you?" Davey asked.

The tall boy pointed to a place beyond the two Ferris wheels. "The funhouse people," he said.

Davey jumped out of his seat. "Oh, boy," he cried. "A funhouse!"

"Make sure you don't miss it," said the tall boy. "I'll see to it that you get a good ride there. I work for the funhouse people."

Then like crumbs being swept away by a dish-towel, the boys were gone.

After they finished their lunch, the Redding family ambled through the amusement park. Brian forgot about the three boys as he walked through the midway, where men and women hawked their games of chance and sold their tickets to the whirling rides.

Mr. Redding bought Davey a big blue ball of cotton candy on a stick. "Do you want one?" he asked Brian.

"I'm full," said Brian.

"I'm never too full for cotton candy," Davey said, his lips stained as blue as a dead person's.

Brian tried his hand at the ring toss. He won a small teddy bear.

Davey grabbed the teddy bear. "I want another cotton candy," he cried.

"You've had enough," Mr. Redding said.

"But it was good," Davey insisted.

Mr. Redding patted his son on the shoulder. "You can have too much of a good thing," he said.

They walked on, still arguing about cotton candy. Ahead loomed the funhouse. Brian's pace slowed. He dreaded running into the three boys from the food stand again.

"Let's go there," Davey cried, pointing to the funhouse.

Brian froze in his tracks.

Mr. Redding got into the ticket line, and they would certainly have gone into the funhouse if it hadn't been for the height requirement.

"There's a roller coaster in this funhouse," the ticket lady explained, "so you have to be at least as tall as that boy." She jerked her thumb in the direction of a wooden figure the size of a boy.

51

Davey rushed over to the figure, which was faded and weather-beaten. Even when he stood on his tiptoes, he was a full two inches too short.

"Guess we'll have to skip this one," Mr. Redding said.

Brian's heart skipped, too. For joy. He felt like his family had dodged a terrible danger. Then he noticed the face painted on the wooden figure. The face was that of one of the three boys from the food stand.

As they turned to leave, Brian saw, from the corner of his eye, the wooden figure move. It crouched down, making itself shorter. Two inches shorter.

"Try again," a thin voice warbled through the wind. "Maybe you grew."

"Let me go stand next to that wooden boy again," Davey suddenly said.

For just a moment, Brian's throat felt very tight.

Mr. Redding laughed. "Maybe next year," he said as he pushed Davey on ahead of him.

It was nearly ten when they rode their last ride. Even then, Davey did not want to leave. "Let's stay for the fireworks," he said, pointing to the grandstand, which was already filling with people.

"I'm too tired," complained Mrs. Redding. "Why don't we go home now? We can watch fireworks on television."

"Fireworks on television?" wailed Davey. "Yuck! What could be more boring than fireworks on television?"

Even Brian, who was tired himself, had to agree

with Davey. So the family climbed to the top of the bleachers and sat down on the rough wooden planks.

At the crack of the first rocket, Davey said, "I have to go to the bathroom."

"Would you mind taking him?" Mrs. Redding asked Brian as a fantail of gold, red, and green cascaded across the sky.

Brian grumbled but followed Davey, who was already running down the steps toward the bathroom. Brian waited outside the long corridor that led to the bathrooms, craning his neck to see the fireworks. He waited and waited. After ten minutes, when Davey still had not returned, he sighed and went into the bathroom to find him.

The bathroom was empty. Davey was gone!

Brian dashed out of the bathroom. At the far end of the corridor, he spied Davey walking with the three boys from the food stand.

"Davey!" The name flew out of the corridor a second sooner than Brian did. He ran into the night, calling after Davey and the boys, but they were running now and were well ahead of him.

Just as they reached the deserted funhouse, Davey turned and called to Brian. "It's okay, Brian. They work here. They said I could ride the roller coaster in the funhouse as long as I want."

The three boys pushed Davey inside the funhouse before Brian could answer.

Brian waded through a wall of fake spider webs into the funhouse after them. Davey and two of the boys were already in the first car of the roller coaster.

The tall boy stood by the controls. He pushed a big lever. The first car lurched forward. "Get out of here," the tall kid called to Brian. "This is a private party. You're not welcome."

In a moment the car with Davey in it would be swallowed up in darkness. Brian dove for the second car as it was pulling away. He rolled into the seat and quickly sat up. Ahead, Davey and the other two boys started to shriek.

The tall boy dropped into the seat beside Brian and pulled the safety bar down across their laps. DON'T RIDE WITHOUT SAFETY BAR IN PLACE read an overhead sign. Somehow, the tall boy's carefulness made Brian feel a little better as they spun off into the darkness.

The first hill hit right away. Exploding butterflies cut through Brian's stomach. Hill followed hill in the madcap darkness. Brian grasped the safety bar tightly. The way it held him securely in place was his only comfort.

"This is great, ain't it," said the tall boy next to Brian. "This is really living."

"Yeah, great," said Brian. "But when is it going to end?"

The tall boy stuck his face so close to Brian's that Brian could smell his foul breath. "That's the very best part," said the tall kid.

The car jolted, slowed, started to inch its way up

a very steep incline. Brian winced, just thinking of the monster hill that must be coming. "What's the best part?" he managed to gasp.

The kid smiled a two-dimensional smile. The kind of smile painted across a canvas, or on a wooden figure of a kid. "The best part is that the ride is never, ever going to end."

Brian tried to push open the heavy lap bar, but it would not budge. The car lurched to the top of the hill, paused a second, then started down. The sinking feeling hit Brian's stomach again. This time it was stronger. Ahead, the shrieks had already begun. Brian threw up his arms and screamed. The rumbling of the roller coaster went on and on, on and on, on and on.

# NIGHT CRAWLER

Mrs. Spiva marched me into the kitchen, her bony fingers pinching my shoulder. "This is our other new boarder. His name is Milford Crowley," she said, introducing me to the old people sitting around the table.

I shuffled my feet uncomfortably. Old eyes gawked at me from around the table. Yellowed eyes in sunken sockets that seemed without hope.

"Just call me Milfy," I said a bit too loudly. "I hate the name Milford."

"Milford is a freshman at the Brainbridge Prep School," said Mrs. Spiva, digging her fingers deeper into my shoulder. "Milford will be staying at the boarding house with us for nine months."

That was only because my parents had spent so much on the tuition for Brainbridge that they couldn't board me there. All they could afford was Mrs. Spiva's run-down boarding house.

"This is Mrs. Durka," said Mrs. Spiva, continuing the introductions.

Mrs. Durka pulled two dark-spotted hands from beneath her shawl. "It's been a long time since we got young boarders," she said. "Now Doc has two to choose from. He will be so happy."

"Hush now, Emma," Mrs. Spiva said, her voice edged with a note of warning. "Don't carry on about Doc. You might say something you shouldn't."

"Do you like cats?" asked Mrs. Kravitz, whose wrinkled hands stroked a gray tabby in her lap.

"I like them, but I'm allergic to them," I said with a sheepish grin.

Mrs. Kravitz held the cat out to me. "This is Kitty Cat. Go on and pet her. She won't take your tongue."

"No, Doc will do that," said Mrs. Durka with an insane titter.

I stumbled back a step and started sneezing. I wanted to ask who Doc was, but I couldn't catch my breath.

"Do you have a girlfriend?" asked Mr. O'Brian, leaning forward and sticking a hand behind one enormous ear to better hear my answer.

"No, I don't," I admitted. "I'm a little shy around girls."

Mr. O'Brian's hand started to shake, whipping his huge ear back and forth. "I had a girlfriend," he said. "Oh, how I miss her. At least you won't have a girlfriend to miss when you get old."

At that moment, Karl Jackman swaggered into

the room. "Doesn't surprise me one bit that you don't have a girlfriend, Crowley," he said with a snort of contempt.

Karl was the football star at Brainbridge. He was only staying at the boarding house while the athletic dorms at Brainbridge were being renovated. I should have liked having him around since he was the only other person at Mrs. Spiva's boarding house under the age of eighty. But I did not like Karl, and he made it known that he did not like me.

Mr. O'Brian patted Karl's back. "Score a touchdown for me in the first game," he said to Karl. "I used to play football, you know. I miss football, too. I miss a lot of things since I got old."

Mrs. Spiva pulled me toward the window. There sat a shapeless bulk with skin the color of freshly peeled potatoes. "And this is Doc," she said.

Doc turned slowly from the window where he had been staring catlike into the sky. He raised one lumpy hand and offered it to me. I shook it. It felt like cold mashed potatoes. The smell that oozed out of the big pores of Doc's skin was like the earthworm smell that sometimes follows a rainstorm.

Doc moved his mouth several times before he was able to mumble, "Looks like rain. That's good, very good. Rain sets the night crawler free to do what has to be done."

The chilling strangeness of Doc's words made me pull my hand from his. It was Monday after-

noon, my first day at the boarding house, and already I felt uncomfortable.

That night, as I warmed a glass of milk in the microwave oven, I overheard Mrs. Kravitz talking to Mrs. Spiva in the hallway.

"Has Doc picked one yet?" Mrs. Kravitz asked.

"Yes, he chose Milford," replied Mrs. Spiva. "It will be so nice having Milford as one of us. He's a good boy."

"Maybe it will rain tonight," Mrs. Kravitz said. "Then the night crawler can come out."

I fled from the kitchen before the two women saw me. Their disturbing conversation was one more reason to suddenly dread rain. When I got to my room, I found myself looking out the window. It looked like rain.

I slipped into bed. The wallpaper in the room seemed to have the same earthworm smell as Doc's skin. I was tossing and turning, when I noticed the spot on the ceiling. The spot was tucked cozily into one corner of the ceiling, and crazy as it seems, I got the idea that it was watching me.

I couldn't sleep that first night. The next morning I stumbled down to breakfast, feeling anything but ready to start my first day at school.

Karl swaggered into the dining room. He pulled the chair out from behind me just as I sat down.

"Gotcha," he said, his mouth twisting into a cruel smile as I fell to the floor.

61

As I picked myself up, Mrs. Spiva bustled in from the kitchen with two platters of bacon and eggs and set them on the table. None of the old people was in the dining room.

Mrs. Spiva picked up a big pitcher and filled two glasses with fresh-squeezed orange juice. Karl grabbed both glasses. "I'm in training," he said.

Mrs. Spiva smiled. "I'll get you another glass, Milford," she said.

As soon as her swirling dress disappeared around the corner, Karl scooped most of my eggs and all but one piece of my bacon onto his plate. I gritted my teeth in silent rage and ate what little he had left me.

Karl had just started to shovel bacon, eggs, and toast into his mouth when Kitty Cat padded into the room, arching her back. Kitty Cat made the unfortunate choice of selecting Karl's leg to rub against while she begged for food.

Karl aimed a vicious kick at the cat that lifted her into the air like a football. Kitty Cat landed in a heap against the far wall. "I thought they were supposed to land on their feet," he said with a grin.

I jumped from my chair and rushed to Kitty Cat. Although she moved a little stiffly, she was soon able to drink some milk and nibble the bacon that I shared with her. As I helped the cat, I realized I had not sneezed. Not once!

I finished what was left of my breakfast with Kitty Cat at my side. As I headed out the door,

Mrs. Spiva came back into the room. "You'd better take your umbrella to school," she said to me. "It looks like rain."

The skin on the back of my neck suddenly felt two sizes too small.

That night the rain came. Remembering Mrs. Spiva's chilling words about Doc choosing me, I crawled under the covers, clicked off the bedside lamp, then clicked it back on again. The room was too gloomy without light. As I listened to the patter of the rain on the old slate roof and thought how soothing the sound of rain usually was, I noticed the spot on the ceiling. Crazy as it seemed, the spot looked bigger tonight. I fought to stay awake. But another night without sleep was more than my tired brain could take. The drumming of the rain on the roof lulled me into an uneasy sleep.

It was only when I heard the odd sucking sound that I realized I was no longer asleep. The earthworm smell was overpoweringly strong now. My skin bunched into gooseflesh. I couldn't bring myself to open my eyes. At last I forced one eye open. Then, I laughed at my silly fears.

I was alone in the room.

I turned my pillow and rumpled it. As I lay my head back down, I looked at the ceiling. The spot had moved. Impossible as it seemed, it had crept halfway between the wall and my bed. And the spot had grown much larger.

*Slurp, slurp . . .*

The sound came from the spot on the ceiling. I almost jumped from my bed. Then an obvious explanation stopped me: The roof leaked.

Of course!

That explained the sucking sound. As for the spot, the rain must have caused it. The spot had moved because the leak was spreading.

The explanation was simple; it was neat. But part of me wouldn't buy it. Part of me insisted on dwelling on some vague fears. Doc had said something about a night crawler coming out when it rained.

Night crawler. Why should the words make my skin crawl? Doc was undoubtedly talking about fishing worms. Everyone knew night crawlers come out when it rains.

Rain beat against the roof. My eyes burned. I wanted to go back to sleep, but I was afraid to.

Then I saw the spot on the ceiling move. It shimmered like the light of a candle in a draft and crept a full inch closer to me.

I watched in horrible fascination. Like a rippling colony of fat earthworms, the spot crept across the ceiling, drawing ever closer to me. Soon it would be directly over me. I don't know why that fact scared me, but it did.

I gasped for air. I wanted desperately to scream, but I remembered Karl Jackman in the next room. He would never let me live it down if I screamed like a baby in the night.

The spot continued to grow as it crawled across

the ceiling. Closer and closer. An inch at a time. And as it moved, it took on a more definite shape. I could almost make it out. But not quite.

A burst of rain hit the roof, then suddenly, all that remained of the rain was the gentle drip, drip, drip of water from the eaves.

An inch at a time, the spot fluttered back to its corner.

I slipped out of bed. I thought maybe I should wake Mrs. Spiva. Or maybe I should call my parents. But get them out of bed at one o'clock in the morning to tell them what? That there was a spot on the ceiling that was trying to get me? That I was afraid of the dark and of the rain?

In the end I did the only thing I could do. I slipped back into bed. But I was determined not to sleep. Sleep, however, stole slowly over me.

How long I slept I don't know. I awoke with a shudder. The earthworm smell was so strong that my stomach heaved. Sweat soaked my bedclothes. Every muscle in my body ached.

It was raining again.

I looked up at the ceiling. The spot was directly over my head. But now the spot had two big eyes—and they were the eyes of Doc.

*Slurp, slurp* . . .

I tried to move, but I could not.

*Slurp, slurp* . . .

The sound was loud, like a radio with the volume pumped up way too loud.

Then the door to the hall swung open, and Kitty Cat tore into the room. With a growl, she sprang straight for the spot on the ceiling.

The spot scurried across the ceiling like a living thing, then with a loud burp it sucked itself back into a flat shape and disappeared into the wall.

Kitty Cat lay next to me and began to purr. I reached over to pet her and discovered that once again my muscles worked. Suddenly a scream echoed through the boarding house. It came from Karl's room. I leaped out of bed and ran into the hallway.

Outside of Karl's room stood the old people. It was only later that I thought to question how they had gotten there so fast.

"Did you hear Karl scream?" I shouted as I threw open his door.

Mrs. Spiva reached out to stop me. "It was just the thunder."

I pulled away from her clutching hands and lurched into Karl's room. I flicked on the light. The earthworm smell, thick as crusted pudding, made me want to retch.

"Where is Karl?" I screamed to the old faces that were bobbing in the doorway like shriveled apples.

Directly above Karl's bed was a gaping hole. Fearing that the ceiling had caved in on him, I rushed to his bed and pulled off the blanket. Wiggling about on his stained sheets was Karl, or at least what remained of him. It was just a jelly

66

outline, but complete down to the tiniest features, wafer-thin features shellacked in fear.

"Help me," cried the transparent mouth. But the pencil-thin plea barely reached my ears when the mass of jelly that had been Karl Jackman started to rapidly age.

In horror I tore down the hall, almost tripping over Kitty Cat. Scooping the cat up like a fumbled football, I dashed down the stairway three steps at a time and out the door.

"Come back," I heard Mrs. Spiva's voice calling. "We can explain everything. You'll get wet out there."

But I didn't listen. With Kitty Cat in my arms, I stumbled through the rain to an all-night convenience store and asked to use the phone. The girl at the counter looked at me like I was crazy, but handed it over. I dialed my parents' phone number.

The phone rang thirteen times before Dad's sleepy voice answered. "Who is this?" he asked gruffly.

I poured out the whole story in gasping sobs. I knew how crazy it sounded, even to me, and I had seen it happen.

"I will check it out," my father said. "Where are you?"

I gave him the address of the convenience store.

I handed the phone back to the girl at the counter. She stood there snapping her bubble gum, like she had seen far stranger things than a kid standing in a convenience store at three o'clock in the morning in soaked pajamas, holding a cat in his arms.

"Thanks," I said.

She blew a bubble, popped it with one finger. "Anytime," she said.

Two hours later, my father pulled into the parking lot. He looked annoyed. "I checked out the boarding house," he said. "Mrs. Spiva tells me you have a runaway imagination."

"What about Karl Jackman?" I asked.

"I met him," my father answered.

"You mean he's all right?"

My father sucked in a long breath of air. "I only hope I'm as spry as Mr. Jackman when I hit my nineties."

"Karl Jackman isn't old!" I shouted. "He's a football player."

My father shook his head. "You must be thinking of that muscular young fellow they call Doc. He's the only young person at the boarding house. Here!" My father handed something to me.

"What is it?" I asked.

"Tickets to Saturday's football game. That nice Mr. Jackman gave them to me. Said he wouldn't be needing them anymore."

# The SQUISHY THING UNDER The BED

On THIS PARTICULAR NIGHT, the picture that hung above Andi Panacci's bed made it impossible for her to sleep. The stormy seashore seemed, well, it seemed too real. Andi could smell the seaweed clinging to the battered rocks. She could taste the salty sea spray. And what were those squishy things the storm had washed onto the shore? Were they sea cucumbers, or something else, something too mysterious to have a name?

Whatever the things were, they made Andi's toes curl just to look at them. She could imagine walking barefoot on that stormy seashore and stepping on one of those squishy things. It would ooze through her toes like lumpy jelly. Of course that could never happen. After all, it was only a picture.

Andi coughed, and even that tasted salty. "Dad, please get me a glass of water," Andi called out.

There was no answer. The house was deathly quiet, except for the noise from the picture. And that was not real noise, just noise inside Andi's head.

"Dad? I want a glass of water."

This time a sleepy voice rumbled from a great distance. "Go to sleep, Andi. Leave your father alone. He has to get up early tomorrow. So do I. So do you."

A new sound filled Andi's room. It was the sound of Andi's teeth grinding together. "Oh, how I hate my stepmother," said Andi. "I wish she were dead. I wish Dad and my real mother would get together again."

Andi looked at the picture. There was plenty of water there. Andi's mother had painted the picture. That's the only reason it hung above Andi's bed.

"Dad! Please get me a drink of water." Andi's voice shook through the walls, making the picture jump in its pink seashell frame. Andi saw something fall from the picture. Something had plopped right out of the picture. It landed on the floor with a thump.

Andi propped her elbows on the edge of the mattress and looked over the side just in time to see something scurry under the bed. A trail of slime marked its path.

Andi screamed.

"Shut up and go to sleep, you little brat," called Andi's stepmother.

Andi screamed again, even louder. Her father mumbled something in response, and Andi heard him stumble out of bed.

"Don't go to her. You'll spoil her rotten," came Andi's stepmother's voice.

Something under the bed bumped into the boxes Andi kept her doll stuff in. Andi's skin tingled the way a cucumber's must when it's doused with vinegar and spices to turn it into a pickle. Her legs ached to jump off the bed and run into her father's room. But she could not bear to touch the slimy carpet with her bare feet.

Then, at the door stood Andi's father. He smiled his bashful smile. "What's the matter, Andi Pancake?" he asked.

"Pancake" made Andi feel better at once. Only her father called her Andi Pancake. To everyone else she was Andi Panacci. "T-there's, there's a squishy thing under my bed," Andi stammered.

"You must have had a dream," Andi's father said.

Andi tossed her hair like a horse's mane. "I was not sleeping."

With a heavy sigh, Andi's father picked up a curtain rod. He knelt beside the bed and poked the rod under it. "Nothing there," he said confidently. "Maybe we should talk a little. Dreams aren't so scary once you talk them out."

Andi opened her mouth to talk, but at that moment the curtain rod stuck to something. Andi's father reached under the bed.

"Don't, Dad . . ." Andi cried.

Something caught hold of Andi's father and pulled him under the bed. A puddle seeped across the carpet, slowly staining it. The squishy thing rolled heavily. It sounded much bigger now.

Andi's stepmother peered into the room. "Where is your father?" she demanded.

Andi pointed under the bed.

Andi's stepmother laughed nervously. "None of your stories, young lady. Where is he?"

Andi looked at her stepmother. "But he really is under the bed. Look for yourself if you don't believe me."

Andi's stepmother pulled up the blanket and stuck her head under the bed. There was a whoosh as she got sucked under, followed by a couple of thumps, then nothing.

The squishy thing rolled out from under the bed. It was very large now. It reared up and towered over Andi.

Andi covered her face with her hands, peeking through her fingers.

The squishy thing waddled to the picture, took hold of the frame and shook it. One by one the other squishy things fell out onto the carpet. There they flopped around like slimy fruit.

Suddenly the big squishy thing spoke to Andi.

Its voice was as squishy as it was. "Things are going to be different around here now," it said.

Andi blinked in confusion. "You can talk."

"I can talk and I can listen," the squishy thing said. "And I seem to remember your asking for a drink."

"Go get Andi a drink," the big squishy thing ordered one of the little squishy things.

The little squishy thing hopped toward the kitchen. In a short while, it returned with a glass of water.

Andi took the glass, but she did not drink. "Where is my father?" she asked.

The big squishy thing pointed to the picture. There in the picture stood Andi's father with Andi's mother, her real mother. "They are together again just as you wished."

Andi Panacci realized that never again would anyone ever call her Andi Pancake. She also realized, a bit belatedly, the wisdom of the old adage "Be careful what you wish for because it just might come true."

# The AFTER-SCHOOL JOB

RICHARD THOMS LEANED HIS BICYCLE against the front of the drugstore. He tried to slick down his stubborn cowlick. It never seemed to want to stay put. Today was no exception.The hair stuck out defiantly, like it was wire and not hair.

Giving up on his cowlick, Richard pulled open the door. It was then that he noticed that the sign was gone. The delivery job he had come to ask about was already taken.

"You going to stand there like a doorman for flies, or are you coming in?" asked a man with heavy jowls, holding a sign in his hands.

Richard let the door hiss shut. "Sorry," he said, making an effort to shoo away a couple of flies that he had let in. "I came about the after-school job. But I see it's already taken."

The man turned over the sign he was holding in

75

his hands. It was the one Richard had seen in the window. "It's yours if you want it," the man said, his beefy jowls quivering.

"The sign?" asked Richard, wondering why the man would think he wanted a sign.

"No, the job. I'm Neville. Neville Ratspat." With this he thrust out a hand to shake with Richard's.

Richard shook the hand firmly. He was surprised at how awkwardly Neville Ratspat shook hands, like he didn't do it much.

"But I thought the job was taken," Richard said, nodding toward the sign. "You already took down the sign, Mr. Ratspat."

"I took the sign down because I saw you coming. Knew right off that you were the right person for the job. And it's just Neville if you please, not Mr. Ratspat."

Richard felt his face blush uncomfortably. He supposed that Mr. Ratspat, Neville that is, was rather sensitive about his odd last name. "I'm sorry," Richard apologized. "I didn't call you by your first name because of your age."

Neville chuckled. "And just how old do you think I am?" he asked.

The question rocked Richard back slightly onto his heels. He had to be careful how he answered it. He remembered the time his Uncle Frank from Sacramento had asked him the same question. Usually jovial Uncle Frank had practically foamed at the mouth when Richard guessed his age to be five years higher than it actually was.

To play it safe, Richard shaved a full ten years off his estimate this time. "I guess you look about fifty," he said at last.

"What if I told you I was younger than you?" Neville said.

Richard smiled. Neville's hair was thinning. His heavy jowls were wrinkled and layered with fat that had taken many hearty meals to accumulate. Oddly though, the rest of him did look quite youthful. The hands that held the sign, for instance, were smooth and spotless.

Richard did not get a chance to answer, however, because at that moment a car swerved noisily to avoid a tiny dog that had wandered onto the street. But the driver was going too fast and struck the little dog, knocking it to the curb in four-pawed cartwheels.

Richard braided his fingers in helpless rage.

Neville placed a hand lightly on Richard's shoulder. "You have a kind heart," he said to Richard. "That is important for the real job that I want you to take."

"I don't understand," Richard muttered. "I thought the delivery job *was* a real job."

Neville shuffled silently behind his counter. He pulled out a box of oil paints and set them onto the counter. Beside the paints he set a paintbrush and a coloring book. The paintbrush was tattered and the coloring book looked generic, without any famous cartoon characters on the cover.

"How would you like the job of caring for the coloring book of last hope?" Neville asked in a hushed tone.

Richard shrugged. "How much does the coloring book job pay?"

"This is the most important job in the world," Neville said. "Please don't take it lightly."

Richard stared at Neville in disbelief.

"I'm not crazy, if that's what you're thinking." Neville looked carefully around him to make sure no one was within earshot. He then spread open the coloring book. "How would you like to be responsible for changing one thing that happens in the world each day?"

Richard looked into the coloring book. He gasped. Miraculously, the scene of the car striking the dog was colored on one of the book's pages. Richard leafed through the book. Other misfortunes from around the entire world covered other pages. Some were too terrible to look at.

"What is this book?" Richard demanded.

Neville quickly shushed Richard. "It's just what I said. A chance to change one bad thing that happens each day, but just one thing mind you, just one."

"Why give the coloring book to me?" Richard asked. "Wouldn't this be a better job for a grown-up, maybe even the President?"

Neville shook his head bitterly. "An adult couldn't handle the job. It takes a fresh, balanced young mind to do it."

Neville picked up the paintbrush and handed it to Richard.

Richard clenched the paintbrush. "What if I was to paint a picture of me getting a million dollars?"

"You won't," said Neville. "I picked you because you care about other people. Your temptation will be to paint more than one change a day. But don't," Neville warned. "Well, do you want the job, or not?"

Richard nodded, his eyes on the book. He was swelling with pride to think that he could actually right things that had gone wrong.

Suddenly, he wanted to ask Neville where the book came from. To ask how Neville had come to get the job, who had it before him. But Neville was nowhere in sight.

A young boy, several years younger than Richard, stepped out from behind the counter. Richard slammed the coloring book shut. He was tempted for just a moment to tell the boy about his power. But he didn't. It would somehow cheapen the job to boast about it. No, the job would remain Richard's secret.

Besides, something about the boy seemed familiar. What was it? Why, the boy resembled Neville. That was it. Must be some relation, Richard thought. Without a word to the boy, Richard put

the coloring book and paints under his arm. Twirling the paintbrush lightly between his fingers, he left the drugstore.

That night, when his homework was done, Richard removed the coloring book from beneath his dresser with trembling fingers and opened it. "Which one, which one?" Richard asked himself over and over.

Richard dwelled for a long time on the unfortunate dog. It seemed more real than the other pictures, perhaps because he had witnessed the accident. In the end, however, Richard painted away a tornado that had killed several people. It had been on the news, and Richard remembered an infant crying in a rescuer's arms. The infant's entire family had died.

When Richard awoke the next morning, he turned on the radio. The news report made him swell with joy. The tornado, it seemed, had miraculously broken up just before it swirled into the community. No one had been hurt.

Richard walked to school. He wondered if anyone could see the importance in his gait or in the finely chiseled features of his face. Could they see in him the goodness of his deed?

Then Richard passed the drugstore. In the gutter by the street lay several tufts of fur where the little dog had died. Richard's gait slowed. He felt the smile slip from his face.

That night Richard made sure that he saved an

animal. Actually, it was an entire herd of beached whales that he saved. Still Richard wasn't happy. It was hard to imagine that so many bad things could happen in a single day. Each night the choice became harder and harder. Richard hardly slept at all.

At last, he reached a bitter conclusion. "I'll paint all the pages tonight," he swore. "I don't care what happens."

And so Richard painted and painted and painted. His head grew heavy, his eyes blurry. Richard threw open the window. The cool air splashed across his face, helping to keep him awake. "This will be a day when no one dies," Richard cried into the night.

The next day, Richard learned the terrible truth. Not one of his colorings had worked. In painting all the pages, it was as though he had painted none. But that was not the worst part. The paint itself had gotten thick. Richard doubted that it could ever be used again.

Frantically, Richard poured different liquids onto the paints. He lined up glass after glass of different substances on his dresser and desk. In his haste, Richard broke a tumbler full of turpentine. The jagged glass tore a ragged cut in his hand. Richard rushed into the bathroom to bandage his hand.

When he returned, Richard felt his back go rigid. There in the bottle where his blood had spilled, there, and there alone, was fresh paint.

Richard undid his bandage and restored each of the other bottles of paint with his own blood. But with each drop of blood that fell from his hand, he grew more and more tired. He felt heavy, sluggish.

Richard looked into the mirror. The face that gazed back at him was old. It had beefy jowls. Richard and the face in the mirror screamed at the same time. Richard gathered up the coloring book, the paints, and the brush. He had to find Neville Ratspat. Maybe it was already too late, but Richard had to know for sure.

Richard dashed into the drugstore. "Is Neville Ratspat here?" he cried to the woman behind the counter.

The woman regarded Richard suspiciously. "He might be," she said. "Who's asking?"

Richard reached over the counter and grabbed the woman's collar in his hands. He shook her none too gently. "Tell me!" he demanded. "Where is he?"

"N-Neville's at soccer practice," she managed to stammer. "P-please don't hurt my little boy."

Richard released the woman. "I don't want your son. I mean old Neville Ratspat."

Now it was the woman's turn to grab Richard by the neck. "There is no old Neville Ratspat," she said. "There's not but one Neville, and he's just a little boy."

The woman pushed Richard back and dashed for the phone. "Hello, police," the woman whined into the phone. "There's a crazy man in my drugstore."

Richard grabbed the paints and headed for the soccer field.

A police car swerved around the bend ahead of Richard. Richard didn't remember if the woman had given the police his description. Taking no chances, he darted into an alley. He knocked over a homeless man rooting through a garbage can.

Suddenly, a young girl loomed in front of him. "You should be ashamed of yourself," the girl scolded Richard as she helped the homeless man to his feet.

The police cruiser nudged slowly into the alley. Richard was about to bolt when he regarded the girl. "You have a good heart," he said to her. "What's your name?"

"Alyson," the girl answered. "And you have to learn to be more careful, mister."

Richard nodded. The police cruiser was getting nearer, its bubble lights splashing red and blue over the faded bricks of the buildings lining the alley. Richard pressed the coloring book into Alyson's hands. He hurriedly explained how it worked. "Do you want the job?" he concluded.

Alyson smiled. She looked at the homeless man. "Just think of all the people I could help."

"But just one a day," Richard reminded her.

Alyson skipped away, book and paints in hand.

The police car squealed to a stop. A policewoman jumped out. "Hold it right there!" she called to Richard.

Richard lowered his head and zoomed off. His legs could only carry him so fast though, and he spilled headlong into an open doorway. In an instant, the policewoman was there. She reached out and grabbed Richard, spun him roughly around.

"Oh, sorry, kid," she apologized. "Did you see an old man run in here? He had a fat face with a double chin."

Richard stared dumbly at the policewoman. "You called me kid," he managed to say at last. Richard patted his face. The folds of fat, the wrinkles were gone.

The policewoman rubbed Richard's head. "Run along now. You shouldn't be hiding in alleys. Why aren't you out playing ball or something normal for kids?"

Richard smiled at the woman. "Maybe I will," he said. "I'll join my buddy Neville down at the field."

The policewoman already had pushed past Richard and was searching the building. Richard thought of Alyson. She would not be playing ball for awhile, he thought. No, she would be much too busy for kid's games. After all, she had the after-school job now.

Al Carusone received a B.S. in geology and an M.A. in teaching from the University of Pittsburgh. He is the author of the popular *Don't Open the Door After the Sun Goes Down* about which *Booklist* wrote, "Teachers, librarians, and parents seeking to meet the never-ending demand for scary stories may find this roundup of nine tales a helpful addition." Mr. Carusone lives in Pennsylvania with his wife and three daughters.

Elaine Clayton is the illustrator of *Six Haunted Hairdos* by Gregory Maguire. A full-time artist, she also writes and illustrates picture books for young children, most recently *Ella's Trip to the Museum* (Crown). Ms. Clayton lives with her family in New Jersey.